To da memories of my brother Ken . . .
forever loved and missed . . .
and Uncle Lawrence . . . you always had faith in me.
MDS

Fe 'Da Tree Mouseketeers' - Greg, Eugenio and Derek,
wid love an' tanks.
GW

First published 2013 by Macmillan Children's Books
A division of Macmillan Publishers Limited
20 New Wharf Road, London N1 9RR
Basingstoke and Oxford
Associated companies throughout the world
www.panmacmillan.com

ISBN: 978-1-4472-1765-7

Text copyright © Michael de Souza and Genevieve Webster 2013
Illustrations copyright © Genevieve Webster 2013
Moral rights asserted.

1 3 5 7 9 8 6 4 2

A CIP catalogue record for this book is available from the British Library.

Printed in China

Rastamouse

and
Da Micespace Mystery

Words by

Michael De Souza & Genevieve Webster

Pictures by

Genevieve Webster

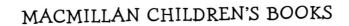

MACMILLAN CHILDREN'S BOOKS

Big up Rastamouse, Scratchy and Zoomer!
Keep it real wid da Easy Crew.
Crime-fighting special agents,
And a ruff, ruff reggae band too.

They're rockin' at Nuff Song studio
And da vibes are sittin' down right.
Da track soundin' super irie,
And da riddim is rollin' tight.

"Mi love da way dat riddim rest,"
Rastamouse says to the Crew.
Zoomer nods in agreement,
And Scratchy says, "Ah, true."

Later, when checking their Micespace page
And uploading the latest song,
Rastamouse says, "Wha 'appen?
Why dis ting takin' so long?"

And just as the upload's about to complete,
The computer starts to flash.
Zoomer cries, "Wait, whaa gwaan?
Mi cyant believe da whole ting jus' crash!"

"Aw man, dat sucks," adds Scratchy,
"Let we all take a break.
We can do dis techie ting laters.
Come on Crew. Let's shake."

Soon they're heading down Grove Street,
Moving so nice an' slick.
Zoomer shouts, "Yo, check dis out!
What ya tink 'bout dis bad boy trick?"

Across town at the orphanage,
The orphans are working hard.
Getting busy with brooms and Bagga T,
Cleaning up the yard.

Later that day when the President arrives,
Excitement fills the place.
But the orphans wonder what could be wrong
When they see the dread look on his face.

"Mi have some bad news," the President says,
"And mi nah know whaa gwaan.
Mi went to da cashpoint machine jus' now
An' all ah da money it gone!

So mi have to postpone da trip for now
An' da pocket money too.
Mi gonna have to call on Rastamouse
To get some help from da Easy Crew."

Meanwhile the Crew reach the skatepark
And this is when they hear
An emergency transmission
Through the radio, loud and clear.

The Crew head out from the skatepark,
Speeding straight for the President's house.
"Oh, tank goodness ya here!" cries Wensley Dale.
"Why? Whaa gwaan?" says Rastamouse.

"All da Mouseland millions gone missin'," says da Prez,
"Nuff dollars widrawn from da bank.
Dis bold-face mouse must be super-bad,
Dat's teefin' ah da highest rank!

When mi reach back, mi print out dis email
But mi nah have no hint of a clue,
Which kinda mouse would do such a ting.
Dat's why me ah call on you."

Rastamouse inspects the email, saying,
"Man dis mouse cheeky for true.
Ya nah worry ya self bout dis any mo'.
Jus' leave it to me an' da Crew."

From: Mi$ter Fl@$h
To: Pre$ident Wen$ley D@le
Subject: Yo!

Yo Pre$ident Wen$ley D@le
FYI: Di$ i$ mi$ter fl@$h.
$orry 2 rin$e out y@
Mou$el@nd @ccount
BTW: T@nk$ 4 d@ c@$h!
Mi needed it 2 upd@te mi ting$
LOL: Me @ expert computer guy
Mi $que@k, me @ geek,
mi got b@re-f@ced cheek
G2G: C-y@. L@ter$.
Goodbye

"Man dat is wicked," laughs Zoomer,
"Dat geek-a-mouse sure is funny."
Scratchy snaps, "Mi nah see da big joke.
Him dangerous! Him teef all dat money!"

So the trio start searching the World Wide Web
And log on to the Micespace site.
Scratchy and Zoomer soon get distracted
But Rastamouse surfs through the night.

"Yo, Easy Crew, come over here.
Jus' take a closer look.
Check out da S's and check out da A's —
Dat must be our cash-teefin' crook!"

So Rastamouse sends out a friend request
Complimenting the expert 'computer guy',
Asking for help with their upload
And this was the speedy reply:

```
From: Mi$ter Fl@$h
To: Da E@sy Crew
Subject: Yo!

Yo E@$y Crew, it would be my ple@$ure
2 help u uplo@d y@ tune
Ju$' hold on deh, me @h go jump inna mi c@r
And mi $ee u at y@ $tudio $oon.
```

So when a super-slick car pulls up outside
The doors rising up on their own,
Out steps a mouse with the thinnest laptop,
MP3, MP4 and an extra-flash phone.

Zoomer shouts, "Mi love dem gadget,
And dat car lookin' kinda new."
"Why, tanks mi bredren," calls the geek-a-mouse,
"FYI, it's a DMW."

Rastamouse greets the bespectacled mouse
And shows him the faulty PC.
In seconds it's fixed and the geek-a-mouse says,
"Dat nah a problem fi a expert like me."

Rastamouse says, "You is da computer king,
Ya know exactly what you ah do.
Jus' like a certain teefin' Mister Flash,
Oh, and BTW, me sure dat is you."

"So tell us why you teef all dat money
Cos me and da Crew keen to hear
Why you rinse out da Mouseland account.
You really tink dat was a great idea?"

"Mi have to confess," says the shame-faced mouse,
"Mi did take 'way all dat cash.
Mi needed to upgrade me gadget and ting.
What can I say? Me is Mister Flash!"

"You'll have to get back all dat money you spent,"
Scratchy says, with a disapproving tone,
"So you'll have to take back dat super-slick car,
Da MP3, MP4 and extra-flash phone."

Rastamouse adds, "Da Crew gonna come,
To make sure ya do tings right.
Mi have to make a call to da President
Den meet me at da orphanage tonight."

So when they meet up later, Rastamouse says,
"Wensley Dale meet Mister Flash.
Dis is da mouse mi was tellin' you 'bout.
Ya know, da one who teef all ya cash."

"So how did you do it?" asks Wensley Dale.
"Dat was easy," says the geek-a-mouse.
"Ya lack of internet bankin' security
Meant me could teef ya from inna mi house."

"Mi tried to log in to da Mouseland account,
It said, 'type in ya password please'.
Mi nah even need da tree attempts,
Mi guess straight way it was 'cheese'."

"It seem clear to us," says Rastamouse,
"You is one very clever guy.
But ya put ya mind to teefin'
And made dem poor likkle orphan cry."

"Dem lose all dem treat," he continued,
"And dem pocket money too.
Mi bredren, if ya give up da teefin'
Mi will fix up da right job for you."

The teefin' mouse listens carefully
To what Rastamouse has to say.
Then he replies with a tear in his eye,
"Mi will stop teefin' from today."

The geek-a-mouse is truly remorseful
So he offers the orphans a treat
Of an extra special day out downtown
And a shopping trip to Grove Street.

He buys them each a criss laptop
And gives them their own special code.
He teaches them about Micespace,
MiTube . . . and of course how to download.

"Remember dat job mi promised you?"
Rastamouse says to the remorseful mouse.
"You can be head of Mouseland security,
And ya can do it from inna ya house."

"Rastamouse! Come in! Come in!
Are you reading me?
Message from President Wensley Dale,
Listen up, you tree.

Ya fix up Mouseland security,
Mi loved ya technical plan.
And ya latest tune is fantastic,
Or as you would say, 'IRIE MAN'!"

GLOSSARY

IRIE
pronounced: i-ree
anything positive or good

NUFF
pronounced: nuhf
enough, a lot

RUFF
pronounced: ruf
great, wicked

CRISS
pronounced: kris
very smart, the best

BREDREN
pronounced: bredrin
a friend, male

ABBREVIATIONS

LOL
laugh out loud

G2G
got to go

C-ya
see ya

MP3/MP4
portable music players

PC
personal computer

BTW
by the way